GOOD DOG, PAW!

Chinlun Lee

WALKER BOOKS
AND SUBSIDIARIES
LONDON • BOSTON • SYDNEY • AUCKLAND

I am Paw.

This is April.

She's my owner.

She's a vet.

Having a vet for an owner is good.
Every morning I have a ten-point check-up
to see if I am healthy all over.

April says,

"ONE,
your eyes,
so bright!

TWO,
your ears, so clean!
No mites
in sight!

THREE, your nose, so shiny!

FOUR, your breath, so sweet! So fresh!

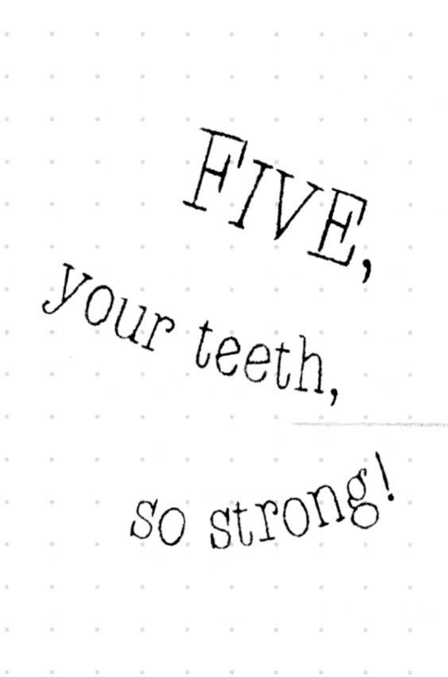

FIVE,

your teeth,

so strong!

SIX,

your paws,

such pads,

such claws!

SEVEN,

your coat,

so warm and furry!

EIGHT,

your tummy,

so soft and

cuddly!

NINE, your tail,
so waggy!

TEN,
the whole of you,
so lovely!

Good dog,
Paw!"

After my check-up,

April does her exercises and I sing a song.

"I am Paw. I love April.

April loves me. I am Paw."

Then we get ready

and scoot to the surgery.

All day, April is
busy, busy, busy.
I sit in my chair and
sing soothing songs to
the animals waiting
to see her.

Poor Jackson the rabbit!

His teeth have grown out of his mouth.

I sing,

"Don't forget to eat your carrots, Jackson.

Carrots, carrots, carrots

keep your teeth short."

My big friend,
Salami the bassett hound,
has a swollen tummy.

I sing,
"Two pills a day will help
those worms away!"

Silver the cat
is bristling with fleas.

I sing,

"My April will dust you,
dust you, dust you with
super-strength flea powder!"

Old Sweet Pea the tortoise
cannot see well.
I sing,

"Don't be afraid, Sweet Pea!
A course of vitamins B, C and A
will soon make your eyes bright again!"

My animal friends like my songs.

They say I know a lot.

But I only know what
April has taught me …

and the best thing
she's taught me is this:

"Love. Love. Love.

Love. Love. Love.

The secret of health is love."

At the end
of the day
April and I
say goodbye to
our last patients.

We play some games,

and go to
the park
for a walk

and a slide.

Then we scoot home

and have dinner.

After dinner we sit together and April gives me a ten-point check-up again.

She says,

"ONE,

your eyes,

so bright!

TWO,

your ears, so clean!

No mites

in sight!

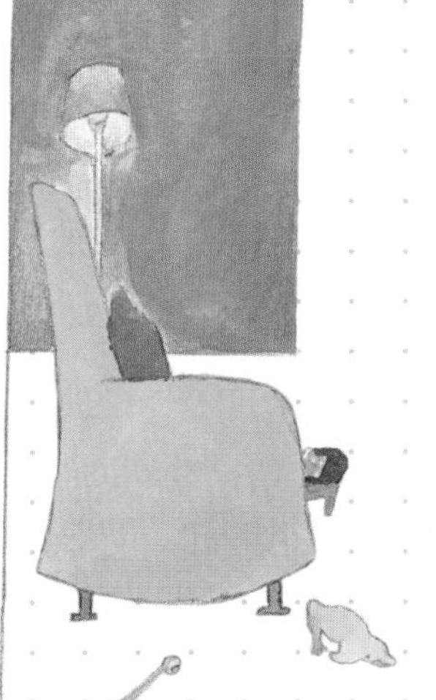

THREE,

your nose,

so shiny!

FOUR, your breath,

so sweet! So fresh!

FIVE,

your teeth,

so strong!

SIX, your paws,

such pads,

such claws!

SEVEN, your coat,

so warm and furry!

EIGHT,

your tummy,

so soft and cuddly!

NINE,
your tail,
so waggy!

TEN,
the whole of you,
so lovely!
Good dog,
Paw!”

April gets ready for bed
and I sing softly to her.

"April, my only April,
how I love you!"

April smiles.

“Good dog, Paw.”